My Family Celebrates
THANKSGIVING

Lisa Bullard

Illustrated by Katie Saunders

LERNER PUBLICATIONS ◆ MINNEAPOLIS

NOTE TO EDUCATORS

Find text recall questions at the end of each chapter. Critical-thinking and text feature questions are available on page 23. These help young readers learn to think critically about the topic by using the text, text features, and illustrations.

Lerner Publications Company
A division of Lerner Publishing Group, Inc.
241 First Avenue North
Minneapolis, MN 55401 USA

For reading levels and more information, look up this title at
www.lernerbooks.com.

Photos on page 22 used with permission of: Joy Brown/Shutterstock.com (turkey); Brent Hofacker/Shutterstock.com (pie); Jordan Adkins/Shutterstock.com (parade).

Main body text set in Billy Infant 22/28.
Typeface provided by SparkyType.

Library of Congress Cataloging-in-Publication Data

Names: Bullard, Lisa, author. | Saunders, Katie, illustrator.
Title: My family celebrates Thanksgiving / Lisa Bullard ; illustrated by
   Katie Saunders.
Description: Minneapolis, MN : Lerner Publications, [2019] | Series: Holiday time
   (Early bird stories) | Includes bibliographical references and index.
Identifiers: LCCN 2017049354 (print) | LCCN 2018011329 (ebook) |
   ISBN 9781541525016 (eb pdf) | ISBN 9781541520097 (lb : alk. paper) |
   ISBN 9781541527430 (pb : alk. paper)
Subjects: LCSH: Thanksgiving Day—History—Juvenile literature.
Classification: LCC GT4975 (ebook) | LCC GT4975 .B854 2019 (print) |
   DDC 394.2649—dc23

LC record available at https://lccn.loc.gov/2017049354

Manufactured in the United States of America
1-44345-34591-3/21/2018

TABLE OF CONTENTS

CHAPTER 1

TURKEY DAY

Gobble, gobble.
My name is Grace, and I'm so excited. Today is Thanksgiving!

It's a holiday for giving thanks.

This year, I'm making a list of what I'm thankful for.

I'm thankful Dad bought such a big turkey!

I'm thankful for dessert too.

I'm also thankful for something else.
I stopped my dog, Zadie, before she ate
all our Thanksgiving pies!

What kind of list is
Grace making?

9

CHAPTER 2
FILL UP WITH FAMILY

Grandpa snuck some pie for himself. But sometimes it's ok to eat dessert first!

I'm happy we have lots of family visiting.

I watch the Thanksgiving parade with my little brother.

I'm thankful for him even though he bugs me sometimes.

What does Grace watch with her little brother?

CHAPTER 3

WHY WE HAVE THANKSGIVING

On TV, they talk about the first Thanksgiving. The people we call the Pilgrims were new to America.

In 1621, they had a three-day feast. They were celebrating good crops. Nearby American Indians helped with these crops. They joined the feast too.

But it wasn't really the first Thanksgiving.

**Yam Festival
(West Africa)**

**Cerealia
(ancient Rome)**

**Sukkot
(Jewish people)**

People around the world have always had days of thanks. Harvest feasts are an old tradition too.

Thai Pongal
(Tamil people)

Crop Over
(Barbados)

Churseok
(Korea)

Mom says I should be thankful for Sarah Josepha Hale. She worked to make Thanksgiving a yearly holiday for the whole country!

Finally, President Abraham Lincoln agreed. He made Thanksgiving a national holiday in 1863.

Why should Grace be thankful for Sarah Josepha Hale?

CHAPTER 4

TIME TO EAT!

It's time to eat! We hold hands and say grace. That's my family's Thanksgiving tradition.

What does Grace's family do when it's time to eat?

I add one more thing to my list. I'm thankful I have a Thanksgiving name—Grace, just like what my family says before Thanksgiving dinner!

LEARN ABOUT HOLIDAYS

Thanksgiving is on the fourth Thursday of November in the United States. Many other countries have different days of thanks.

Food is a big part of Thanksgiving. Many people eat turkey. Some people also serve meals to those who don't have enough to eat.

Pies are a popular Thanksgiving dessert. Pumpkin pie, apple pie, and pecan pie are three common kinds.

Many people travel to see family for Thanksgiving. Some fly or drive long distances. It's one of the busiest travel times of the year.

Many places have Thanksgiving parades. The most famous is Macy's Thanksgiving Day Parade. It takes place in New York City and features giant balloons.

THINK ABOUT HOLIDAYS: CRITICAL-THINKING AND TEXT FEATURE QUESTIONS

Why do you think Thanksgiving was made a holiday?

What are some things you are thankful for?

How many pages are in this book?

What chapter starts on page 14?

LERNER

SOURCE™

Expand learning beyond the printed book. Download free, complementary educational resources for this book from our website, www.lerneresource.com.

GLOSSARY

American Indians: the first people to live in America

crop: a plant that is grown for food

grace: a prayer said at a meal

harvest: a time when vegetables, fruits, or grains are ready to be picked and eaten

Pilgrims: a name later given to a group of people from England who arrived in America in 1620 and settled at Plymouth Bay in Massachusetts

tradition: a belief or action handed down over time

TO LEARN MORE

BOOKS
Dean, Kimberly, and James Dean. *Pete the Cat: The First Thanksgiving.* New York: HarperCollins, 2013. Join Pete the Cat as he learns all about the first Thanksgiving.

Fearing, Mark. *The Great Thanksgiving Escape.* Somerville, MA: Candlewick Press, 2014. Gavin and his cousin Rhonda are at their grandma's for Thanksgiving. Follow them as they try to make it past their relatives and to the swing set.

WEBSITE
Thanksgiving Crafts and Children's Activities
http://www.dltk-holidays.com/thanksgiving/index.html
Find lots of great Thanksgiving activities at this fun website!

INDEX